FIGHT CLUB 2 ™

FIGHT CLUB 2 ™

The Tranquility Gambit

Story by
CHUCK PALAHNIUK

Art by
CAMERON STEWART

Colors by
DAVE STEWART

Letters and logo by
NATE PIEKOS OF BLAMBOT ®

Cover and chapter break art by
DAVID MACK

Dark Horse Books

President and Publisher . . . . Mike Richardson
Editor . . . . Scott Allie
Associate Editor . . . . Shantel LaRocque
Assistant Editor . . . . Katii O'Brien
Designers . . . . Rick DeLucco, Ethan Kimberling
Digital Art Technician . . . . . . Christianne Goudreau

This book is dedicated to my fellow workshop writers, many of whom have lent their likenesses to the project—Chelsea Cain, Monica Drake, Erin Leonard, Diana Jordan, Suzy Vitello, Mary Wysong-Haeri, and Lidia Yuknavitch.—CP

This book first came into being over a delicious dinner cooked by Marc Mohan.

Special thanks to Matt Fraction, Chelsea Cain, Kelly Sue DeConnick, Brian Michael Bendis, Todd Doughty, and Edward Hibbert.

Neil Hankerson, Executive Vice President / Tom Weddle, Chief Financial Officer / Randy Stradley, Vice President of Publishing / Nick McWhorter, Chief Business Development Officer / Matt Parkinson, Vice President of Marketing / Dale LaFountain, Vice President of Information Technology / Cara Niece, Vice President of Production and Scheduling / Mark Bernardi, Vice President of Book Trade and Digital Sales / Ken Lizzi, General Counsel / Dave Marshall, Editor in Chief / Davey Estrada, Editorial Director / Chris Warner, Senior Books Editor / Cary Grazzini, Director of Specialty Projects / Lia Ribacchi, Art Director / Vanessa Todd-Holmes, Director of Print Purchasing / Matt Dryer, Director of Digital Art and Prepress / Michael Gombos, Director of International Publishing and Licensing / Kari Yadro, Director of Custom Programs

Published by Dark Horse Books
A division of Dark Horse Comics, Inc.
10956 SE Main Street
Milwaukie, OR 97222

First edition: June 2016
ISBN 978-1-61655-945-8

Limited edition: June 2016
ISBN 978-1-50670-230-8

First paperback edition: May 2018
ISBN: 978-1-50670-628-3

10 9 8 7 6 5 4 3 2 1
Printed in China

International Licensing: (503) 905-2377
Comic Shop Locator Service: comicshoplocator.com

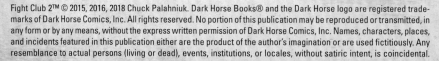

This edition collects Fight Club 2 #1–#10 and the Fight Club 2 Free Comic Book Day 2015 story.

Library of Congress Cataloging-in-Publication Data

Names: Palahniuk, Chuck, author. | Stewart, Cameron, 1976?- illustrator. | Stewart, Dave, illustrator. | Piekos, Nate, illustrator. | Mack, David, 1972- illustrator.
Title: Fight Club 2 : the tranquility gambit / story by Chuck Palahniuk ; art by Cameron Stewart ; colors by Dave Stewart ; letters and logo by Nate Piekos of Blambot ; covers and chapter break art by David Mack.
Other titles: Tranquility gambit
Description: First edition. | Milwaukie, OR : Dark Horse Books, 2016.
Identifiers: LCCN 2015049534 | ISBN 9781616559458 (hardback)
Subjects: LCSH: Young men--Comic books, strips, etc. | Hand-to-hand fighting--Comic books, strips, etc. | Self-actualization (Psychology)--Comic books, strips, etc. | Graphic novels. | BISAC: COMICS & GRAPHIC NOVELS / Media Tie-In. | GSAFD: Comic books, strips, etc.
Classification: LCC PN6727.P347 F54 2016 | DDC 741.5/973--dc23
LC record available at http://lccn.loc.gov/2015049534

INTRODUCTION

I didn't see this coming. Any of it.

Let's go back to sometime around 1995. I was working as an editor at the firm of W. W. Norton, a proudly independent and employee-owned New York house best known to the public as the publisher of *The Norton Anthology of English Literature*. A pretty conservative place, but one that also gave an editor his head if he didn't ask for a lot of money. I had read a novel in manuscript by a guy with the hard-to-pronounce name of Chuck Palahniuk with the title *Invisible Monsters*, about a horribly maimed supermodel bombing around the Pacific Northwest with some phony Eurotrash friends, stealing drugs from the cabinets of the rich and elderly, selling half of them at the local bars and gobbling up the rest. The hysterical voice of the novel drove me crazy (in a good way), but I couldn't quite understand what was really going on in the book and so could not quite get my colleagues, who were much less charmed, to let me make an offer to publish.

But as it turned out, this Chuck guy came to New York for a visit soon after, and I met him and liked him. He wore checked flannel just like someone from Portland, Oregon, should, and he had a dry and offbeat sense of humor. We later met again at a perfectly horrible writers' conference in Everett, Washington, and that time he was wearing a white Prince Valiant-y shirt with puffed-out sleeves remarkably like the famed puffy shirt worn by Jerry Seinfeld. We corresponded after that, and one day he sent me a story titled "Fight Club," about white-collar drones who head to a certain bar on weekends to pound each other into near-oblivion as a way to escape the consumerist/office-job blues. They head back into work on Monday with ominous bruises and wobbling teeth, and nobody screws with them anymore. They feel *alive*. It was outrageous and perfectly done, and Chuck asked me if I thought he should develop it into a novel. Uh, yeah.

In time the complete manuscript of *Fight Club* arrived at Norton from his agent, Edward Hibbert, and it was unnerving and anarchic and just brilliant. I thought that Chuck had developed his premise with enormous inventiveness and convincing, if occasionally baroque, detail (the things you can learn as Chuck's editor . . .). I bought, totally bought, the book's thesis that contemporary young men suffered from an absence of strong male role models and the malaise of meaningless work and hamster-wheel consumption at Ikea and the Gap, and that only regeneration through violence could bring them back to spiritual life. It made sense to me. I was in. But as for the question every book editor has to ask himself, "Who is going to buy it?" my honest answer to myself had to be "Fucked if I know." You needed a somewhat depraved sense of humor and a pretty strong stomach to go where Chuck was taking you. It sure wasn't like anything else being published in the mid-nineties. That's what I liked about it.

I still vividly remember the editorial meeting where I brought *Fight Club* up for acquisition. The odds were not good. None of my other readers save one assistant, bless her, expressed any enthusiasm—in fact there was mostly an ominous silence, although one editor did say to me, ambiguously, "Well, *you're* good at this sort of thing." That was either a compliment or an indictment. I made my pitch for the book as best I could, to be greeted again by silence around the conference table, which I interpreted, correctly I'm sure, as my colleagues thinking, "He's nuts, but I'm going to let someone else knock him over." With mere seconds to go before that happened, I blurted out, "Look, I really think there's something going on here. Just give me $6,000 to offer and I won't come back to you, I promise." To which the kindly president of the company replied, "Oh, let the kid have his book." (I was forty-five at the time.) I said thanks and rushed to my office to make the offer before they could take it back. And it was accepted.

(Chuck has referred to that offer in print as "fuck-you money." I respectfully disagree. What it was was "Well, okay . . ." money.)

I then proceeded to edit the book, in a couple of key cases getting Chuck to dial back a bit of the violence and darkness. As in not having the sheriff actually castrated in the men's room, just threatened with castration. (So glad that change was made when I saw that scene in the movie . . .). But here is a slightly embarrassing admission I've never made in public before: I did not realize that Tyler Durden was just a projection of the narrator's splintering psyche. I thought he was an actual character because, in my defense, Marla also talked directly to Tyler, and how could another person believe in someone's hallucination? So I convinced Chuck to make the changes necessary to correct what I thought was a source of potential reader confusion. Marla always talks to the narrator, not to Tyler.

I do want to state that Norton published *Fight Club* with genuine enthusiasm. The sales force really took to the book and we sold paperback rights for $25,000, so it was a financial success right out of the box. To this day I hear from editors who worked at paperback houses when *Fight Club* came up for discussion and opinions were violently divided on its merits or lack thereof. "So you're the guy who edited that book," they say with guarded respect. The book received some favorable reviews and some hostile ones, and a certain culty buzz gathered about it, but the sales in hardcover were modest—5,000 copies at most. But Chuck was genuinely launched and I was able to sign up his next novel, one of my favorites, *Survivor*. A modest victory against the forces of consensus reality, I thought.

And then *Fight Club* took on a miraculous second life in Hollywood. A powerful producer at Fox, Laura Ziskin, decided to option it for film, God knows why. Jim Uhls wrote a fantastic script, one of the best book-to-film adaptations ever penned. David Fincher, the dark lord of the cinema, took the project on with the fervid commitment of a personal crusade and made a film so visceral and unsettling that Fox postponed its release until many months after the massacre at Columbine. The theatrical release was deemed a commercial failure, but the DVD with its many extras and endless broadcasts on Spike and other cable channels have had their effect, and *Fight Club* is now recognized as a generational classic and almost a literary rite of passage. Chuck has gone on to write many more challenging novels of unsurpassed inventiveness and wicked humor that have sold millions of copies around the world. One of them was *Invisible Monsters*, which my formerly cautious colleagues at Norton picked up; the rest I have had the keen pleasure of publishing myself. His days as an assembly line worker and technical writer at the Freightliner Corporation are a distant memory. *Fight Club* is a staple of men's studies. And at a certain point I stopped clipping out puns on *Fight Club*'s title and "The first rule . . ." allusions because why bother? On the evidence, I guess I am "good at this sort of thing." Damn right I am.

And now *Fight Club*, in this sequel, has made the transition to a medium that feels like it might have been invented to accommodate the genius and wit of Chuck Palahniuk. Just another thing I didn't see coming, but I'm so glad it has arrived. Tyler Durden lives!

— Gerald Howard
October 2015

FIGHT CLUB 2 ™

The Tranquility Gambit

LOOK UP AND YOU'RE GONE.

THERE USED TO BE MAPLE FLOORING.

NOW THERE ARE TRACES OF POTASSIUM PERCHLORIDE.

IN THIS FILING CABINET FOR WIDOWS AND YOUNG PROFESSIONALS.

UTION – DO NOT CRO

AND I USED TO BE SUCH A NICE PERSON.

STEP OVER THE EDGE.

JUMP OVER THE EDGE.

IT'S NOT CANCER.

Marla Calling

THOSE CHANGES IN MY BREASTS.

I NEED TO SEE YOU.

I'M BEING FOLLOWED.

IT'S THURSDAY.

SLIDE...

PICTURE YOUR BOWEL CANCER AS A BALL OF BRIGHT, HEALING LIGHT...

PICK SOMEONE VERY SPECIAL TO YOU, TONIGHT.

HSSS

SO YOU'RE BOTH IN REMISSION?

HE'S **NEVER** HAD CANCER. HE ONLY COMES HERE TO TRICK PEOPLE INTO **LOVING HIM!**

WELL, SHE ONLY COMES HERE BECAUSE YOUR **CANCER** MAKES HER FEEL BETTER ABOUT HER OWN **LOUSY, WASTED LIFE!**

HE'S BEEN FOOLING YOU FOR **YEARS!**

HELLO my name is Hamish

HELLO my name is LA TROYZ

HELLO my name is XAVIER

HELLO my name is CHANG

HELLO my name is Running Wolf

YEAH, FULL-BLOOD NAVAJO.

HE'S NOT DYING! HE'S NOT EVEN A NAVAJO!

BAM BAM BAM

WE'RE CLOSED!

FIGHT CLUB CELL NUMBER 458, OPEN UNTIL FIVE A.M., PASSWORD "CORNFLOWER BLUE."

I KNOW THIS BECAUSE TYLER KNOWS THIS.

MR. DURDEN, SIR!

GET ME THE LIST!

I'M PULLING RANK.

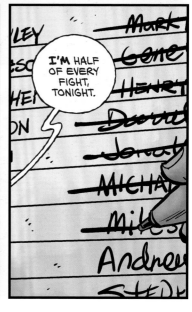

I'M HALF OF EVERY FIGHT, TONIGHT.

YOU'VE HEARD OF "DEATH BY COP"...?

NEXT!

...THIS WOULD BE "DEATH BY FIGHT CLUB."

CLUNK

ARISE, LAZARUS!

I'M DEAD.

YOU'RE NOT DEAD.

YOU QUITTER!

YOU DON'T HAVE MY PERMISSION TO DIE.

YOU NEED TO DIE A **HERO'S** DEATH.

WAIT!

THTAY BAGK!

DEATH TO COMMENCE IN TEN...NINE...

EVERYTHING IS GOING TO BE **FINE!**

EIGHT... SEVEN...

THE **BUILGIN'** ITH GONNA ETHPLODE!

SIX... FIVE...

THIS 'HO' BUILGIN' ITH ABOU' A ETHPLODE!

DON'T WORRY.

EVERYTHING IS GOING TO BE ALL RIGHT.

THE END

AFTER THE HONEYMOON:
A RATIONALIZATION

Tyler didn't die. The original novel died. It sold fewer than 5,000 copies in hardcover. The film died, lasting less than two weeks in theaters. As the head of marketing for 20th Century Fox told director David Fincher, "Congratulations. You've made a movie with so much blood no woman will watch it, and so much male nudity no man will." But Tyler, he went into the world, and he spread by word of mouth. Yes, like an infection.

According to Victor Turner and Arnold van Gennep this had to happen. A little Anthropology 101, here. To be transformed, a person must leave the world and return. Turner's favorite example was the honeymoon trip. A couple is wed in a public ceremony. They leave their community for a time. And only when they return are they recognized as fully married. That's why so many classic stories include a road trip at their hearts. In *One Flew Over the Cuckoo's Nest*, it's the fishing trip that prompts Billy Bibbit's suicide. Think of the road trip in *The Great Gatsby*. All the characters drive into New York City, to the Plaza Hotel where they drink gin while Mendelssohn's Wedding March roars up from a ceremony on the floor below. On the drive home Daisy kills her husband's mistress, and everything falls to pieces.

According to van Gennep—who coined the term "rite of passage"—it's why Jesus Christ had to be publically crucified and dwell three days in the land of the dead before he could be resurrected to glory.

And it's why Jonah had to cool his heels three days in the belly of the whale before he could bring salvation to Nineveh.

It's why my first three novels all include a road trip in the second act—the characters leaving the *mise en scène* only to discover their own true natures. Most notably the nameless narrator of *Fight Club,* hunting the world to find himself.

To recognize his world—and to be recognized by it—a person must leave his peers, be away, and finally return home.

So Tyler Durden didn't die. In Ireland and Brazil and Ukraine, he recruited. His voice became the discourse of today's politics with all its talk about "snowflakes" and the Antifa's college-based "fight clubs" for training members in how to punch a Nazi. It's the video of Richard Spencer being sucker punched in the ear. We hear Tyler in the headlines of Paul Kersey when he reports interracial crime by writing, "Her name is..." and in the characters chanting the same on the cable comedy *Workaholics* (a favorite ... website What Would Tyler Durden Do...

His words echo from the ... old "Kindergarten Fight Club" of New ... to the proposed fight club in the ... *Bridesmaids*, to Nike's "Flight Club" line ... sports apparel.

In no way did Tyler die.

He's rallied his troops from the political left and right. And now Tyler's so big he's almost unrecognizable. Victor Turner would be so proud.

Now Tyler Durden is everywhere.

LOOK AT HIM. HE CALLS HIMSELF **SEBASTIAN** THESE DAYS.

TEN YEARS AGO HE WAS DESTINED TO BE ANOTHER ALEXANDER THE GREAT. A NEW GENGHIS KHAN. BUT **SEBASTIAN**...

HE CALLS HIMSELF HAPPY.

HIS SHIELDS AGAINST THE SLINGS AND ARROWS OF EVERYDAY LIFE.

HE TRADED HIS ARMY... FOR WHAT?

HAPPY ANNIVERSARY, SIR.

NO CHARGE. NOT FOR YOU, SIR.

DESTINY HAS A PESKY WAY OF CATCHING UP.

I'M NOT ME.

MARLA, I'M HOME!

2:58pm

Reminder
Hope For Tomorrow
First Congregational
Church - 3:00pm

NO, OFFICER, I'M JUST THE BABYSITTER... YES, A CRAZED MAN JUST BURST THROUGH THE FRONT DOOR...

IS THAT MY MEDICAL MARIJUANA?

SNIF

BEATS ME, WHERE MARLA GOES EVERY AFTERNOON.

?

"SHE'S YOUR WIFE."

HE SEARCHES HER SEARCHES OF HIS SEARCHES OF HER SEARCHES...THE CHATROOM THREADS OF AN UNRAVELING MARRIAGE.

History   Book

Show History

Reopen Last C

Colon Cancer
Hepatitis
Cirrhosis
Sickle Cell An
Multiple Scler
Achondroplas

THIS IS "PRO-JERRY-AH," RIGHT?

MARLA SINGER. THE FACE THAT LAUNCHED A THOUSAND TRIPS TO THE E.R.

IT'S "HUTCHINSON-GILFORD PROGERIA SYNDROME."

YOU'RE IN THE WRONG PLACE.

26

PROGERIA **SYNDROME** IS A RAPID ACCELERATION OF THE AGING PROCESS CAUSED BY A DEFECTIVE GENE UNABLE TO INTERACT CORRECTLY WITH PROTEINS--

I HAVE THAT.

I AM ELEVEN YEARS OLD.

I'LL BE NINE NEXT MONTH.

WELL, I HAVE A VERY MILD CASE.

JUST **LOOK** AT ME! I'M THIRTY-FIVE YEARS OLD, BUT I COULD PASS FOR **FIFTY!**

MY WRINKLES-- THEY'RE ALL ON THE **INSIDE!**

I KNOW ALL ABOUT ACCELERATED PREMATURE AGING. TODAY IS MY NINTH WEDDING ANNIVERSARY, BUT I COULD SWEAR I'VE BEEN MARRIED FOR SIXTY YEARS!

I'M SO TIRED OF DIETING AND COLORING MY HAIR.

I JUST WANT TO GET FUCKED FOR WHO I AM!

ME, TOO.

THAT'S INAPPROPRIATE SEXUALIZED LANG--

LOOSEN UP, GIRLFRIEND. BIOLOGICALLY SPEAKING, YOU'RE TWO HUNDRED YEARS OLD.

HE WASN'T ALWAYS SO BORING...

I WAS DYING OF A DRUG OVERDOSE, AND HE FUCKED ME BACK TO LIFE!

HE GAVE ME ORGASMS THAT SHAVE YEARS OFF YOUR LIFESPAN!

WHAT'S AN ORGASM?

I WAS THE **REAL** CRAZY PERSON.

I THOUGHT I COULD FIX HIM.

OUR LITTLE BOY IS NINE YEARS OLD.

DOES HE LIKE LEGOS?

I'LL BE NINE NEXT APRIL...IF I LIVE THAT LONG.

MY MARRIAGE ISN'T GOING TO LIVE UNTIL NEXT APRIL.

I WISH I'D NEVER MET HIM--

SLAM

CLICK

CAN YOU MOW THE LAWN BEFORE DINNER?

WHAT DID YOU DO THIS AFTERNOON?

REMEMBER WHAT TODAY IS?

HAPPY ANNIVERS

I LO YOU

TAKE YOUR PILL.

THROUGHOUT CHILDHOOD PEOPLE TELL YOU TO BE LESS SENSITIVE.

ADULTHOOD BEGINS THE MOMENT SOMEONE TELLS YOU, "YOU NEED TO BE **MORE SENSITIVE.**"

BARK

WHEN SEBASTIAN MET MARLA SINGER, HIS HEART BEGAN TO...

BARK

BUT BY THE TIME HIS SON WAS BORN, THE DRUGS HAD SHUT IT JUST AS FA...

BARK BARK

BARK

BARK

CHEMISTRY Experiment Set

Holy Bible

NOW SEBASTIAN IS THE FATHER HE'D VOWED NEVER TO BECOME. DETACHED. DISCONNECTED BY THE DRUGS...

BARK

WHERE DO I GET AMMONIUM SULFIDE?

BARK BARK

BARK

BARK

SPLORK

BARK BARK

IT'S MR. COFFEY.

BARK BARK BARK

MR. COFFEY THROWS THEIR DOG POOP OVER.

BARK

WHY DID YOU COME HOME EARLY?

DINNER'S ON THE TABLE.

DADDY DIDN'T COME HOME EARLY.

YOU WERE NAPPING.

BARK

BUT I HEARD YOU.

YOU WERE DREAMING.

TRACY TOLD MOM YOU HAD FLOWERS...

WASH UP AND GET IN HERE!

BARK

TELL YOUR MOTHER I WENT NEXT DOOR.

BARK

YOU'D BETTER NOT.

COFFEY!

BARK BARK

BARK

BARK

BARK

BELIEVE IT OR NOT, YOUR OLD MAN USED TO LOVE A GOOD FIGHT.

WITH INSOMNIA, EVERYTHING FEELS LIKE A COPY OF A COPY OF A COPY.

BARK

BARK

BARK

TYLER...

BARK

TYLER... DELIVER ME FROM THIS BLAND, BORING LIFE.

BARK BARK

BARK BARK

MARLA LOOKS LIKE SHE'S DIED AND GONE TO HEAVEN.

BARK BARK

6:00 AM BZZZT

WAKE UP.

OBJECTIVE

RogueKnight

L4z3rbo

30/150

DR. WRONG? CAN YOU SEE ME THIS AFTERNOON?

UNDER AND BEHIND EVERYTHING THE MAN TOOK FOR GRANTED, SOMETHING HAD BEEN GROWING.

AH, DOC, WE'VE GOT TO STOP MEETING LIKE THIS!

OH BALLS!

IT'S YOUR FRANKENSTEIN MONSTER...

...I'M BAAAAACK!

DRAT.

Call Ended

MR. DURDEN, WELCOME.

YOUR GLASSES, DOC. FORK OVER YOUR SPECS.

SEBASTIAN IS PRACTICALLY BLIND!

I'D LIKE THE FOLLOWING PERSONS KILLED AS PER USUAL-- QUICKLY AND WITHOUT SUFFERING.

RIZE OR DIE INTERNATIONAL

TANZANIA IN-COUNTRY REBEL UNIT #17

PIRANESI SPANISH INDIGENOUS FREEDOM FIGHTER SQUAD #14

A CAR BOMB OUGHT TO GROW OUR BUSINESS IN TUNIS.

WE'LL SEE IF BRAZIL STILL WANTS TO CUT ITS MILITARY BUDGET AFTER THIS...

SOAP SALES, I'M HAPPY TO SAY, ARE THROUGH THE ROOF!

FOR FIFTY MINUTES, THREE TIMES EACH WEEK OVER THE PAST TEN YEARS...

...I'VE BEEN EMERGING TO RUN THE WORLD.

IS TONIGHT'S ASSASSINATION STILL A GO?

MY ENTIRE TEAM IS PREPPED.

AND YOUR SON, SIR? NO REGRETS?

REMEMBER, DOC--I'M NOT SEBASTIAN.

THE BITCH IS NOT MY WIFE...

BARK BARK

BARK BARK

THE KID'S NOT MY KID.

OH, TYLER...

DELIVER ME FROM THIS LOVELY TRAP.

BARK

BARK BARK BARK

PLEASE, RESCUE ME FROM MY LOVING HUSBAND...

HE IS NEVER GOING TO BE A MOVIE STAR OR A ROCK GOD. WORSE, HE IS NEVER GOING TO BE YOUNG AGAIN. NOW, **AFTER** THAT FIGHT, HE KNOWS SOMETHING HAS CHANGED.

COFFEY!

STUDIES CONDUCTED BY THE UNITED STATES MILITARY PROVE THAT WHAT WOMEN FEAR MOST IS PHYSICAL PAIN...

...WHAT MEN FEAR MOST IS BEING HUMILIATED, LOSING SOCIAL STATUS, PUBLIC RIDICULE.

YOU'RE HERE, SO I MUST BE...

ASLEEP.

WHY HAVE YOU COME BACK?

TO SAY GOOD-BYE.

THE SAME WAY I TOLD YOUR FATHER GOODBYE.

THE FIRE INSPECTOR SAID...

ARSON.

TRACES OF...

...HOMEMADE POTASSIUM NITRATE.

HOW DÉJÀ VU.

OVER HERE!

THEY FOUND A...

49

OUR SON.

THANKS.

THE RED CROSS HAS US IN A MOTEL.

TOMORROW, THE INSURANCE ADJUSTER...

WE NEED TO GET YOU BACK ON YOUR MEDICATIONS.

FIRST, SOME HYPNOSIS.

WHO WOULD DO THIS?

NO HYPNOSIS.

HE HADN'T CRIED SINCE TAKING

THE POSSIBLE DEATH DOES RAISE A RED FLAG.

SHEILA HOLMAN
SENIOR ADJUSTER

POSSIBLE?

YOU TOOK OUT SUCH A LARGE POLICY...

...ONLY DAYS AGO.

LIFE INSURANCE?

WE DIDN'T.

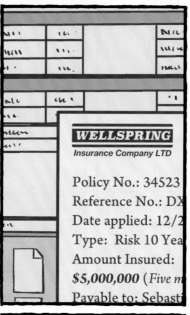

WELLSPRING
Insurance Company LTD

Policy No.: 34523

Reference No.: DX

Date applied: 12/2

Type: Risk 10 Yea

Amount Insured:

$5,000,000 (*Five m*

Payable to: Sebast

YOU INSURED YOUR CHILD A WEEK AGO, ONLINE, AT 4:17 A.M.

HOW?

WE WERE ASLEEP.

IN LIGHT OF THE F.B.I.'S REPORT, THE POLICY IS MOOT.

F.B.I.?

SO IT WASN'T ARSON?

DEPARTMENT of INVESTIGATION
FBI

CHERRY JOB.

SOME HEADHUNTER RECRUIT YOU IN THE LOONY BIN?

WE UNDERSTAND YOU'RE ON A LOT OF MEDICATION.

YOU THINK ABOUT YOUR FATHER MUCH?

WHAT BEARING--

WHERE IS YOUR OLD MAN?

DIED IN A FIRE.

AND YOUR MA?

BOTH DIED IN A FIRE?

DIFFERENT FIRES.

BELOVED MOTHER

INSURANCE PAY FOR COLLEGE?

ALMOST A MERCY KILLING.

BELOVED MOTHER

BELOVED FAT

IT WAS ARSON, ALL RIGHT.

JOHN ROA
FIRE MARSHAL

KNOW A RAUL KENSINGTON SEYMOUR?

POOR RAUL. HIS M.CATS SHOWED SUCH PROMISE.

A SECOND-YEAR MED STUDENT.

YOU SUSPECT HIM?

BOTCHED HIS MIDTERMS.

"SWEATING BULLETS TO BOOST HIS G.P.A."

I REALIZE THAT, MR. DURDEN.

"TWO WEEKS AGO, HE DISAPPEARED..."

I HAVE A THREE POINT TWO!

"IT WAS **HIS** BURNT BODY."

BOTH HAD SCARS. **OLD** SCARS.

A STIGMATA IS A STIGMATA.

THE F.B.I. SAYS TO STAY PUT.

THEY WEREN'T MY PARENTS.

THEY'D SERVED THEIR PURPOSE IN HISTORY.

I WAS COMPELLED TO RESOLVE THEM.

I WORE THIS MONKEY SUIT AT HIS WEDDING.

CORRECTION: WEDDINGS.

I, HERBERT, TAKE YOU, EVA--

...TAKE YOU, NADJA--

...TAKE YOU, TWANDA--

...TAKE YOU, MAY LING--

...TAKE YOU, ESPERANZA--

NO OFFENSE, BUT I HAD A DIFFERENT SET OF STEPSIBLINGS EVERY CHRISTMAS...

MI PADRE ES SU PADRE.

BRIIIIIIIIINNG

I'M GOING TO NEED...

I LIED.

ABOUT THE SUPPORT GROUP?

I'M HAVING AN AFFAIR.

WITH COFFEY?

WHO?

OUR NEIGHBOR.

UGH! NO!

THEN WHO?

I CUT YOUR MEDS A LITTLE--

TYLER?

64

TECHNICALLY, THAT'S NOT ADULTERY--

ARE YOU CRAZY?

I'M NOT THE SPLIT PERSONALITY!

YOU KNEW HE WAS DANGEROUS!

I KNOW.

MY POINT IS, I KNOW SOME PEOPLE.

THEY KNOW ALL ABOUT COMPUTER HACKING.

THEY'RE DESPERATE TO SAVE ANOTHER CHILD...

OURS.

HIDE OUT. YOU CAN'T BE TAKEN AS A HOSTAGE.

STEER CLEAR OF ANYBODY WITH BRUISES OR MISSING TEETH-- GOT IT?

I'LL NEED BETTER CREDENTIALS THAN THIS...

I WANT YOU TO HIT ME AS HARD AS YOU CAN.

BABY, I'M SO SORRY!

WHY DO WE LOVE PEOPLE THE MOST THE MOMENT **AFTER** WE HURT THEM?

SORRY BECAUSE YOU **HIT** ME, OR BECAUSE YOU'RE A TWO-TIMING **WHORE?**

HOW ABOUT YOU BEAT ME UP WITH THIS?

HOLY BIBLE

Holy Bible

TOO FRAUGHT.

WITH THIS?

YOU'RE BLEEDING. THEY'RE PRADA.

IF IT HELPS MOTIVATE YOU, I KNOW WHO KIDNAPPED OUR CHILD.

TELL ME.

I COULD BASH IN YOUR **BRAINS.**

NOW WE'RE GETTING SOMEWHERE!

I HAVE AN IDEA.

STAND IN THE BATHTUB. THIS WILL GET MESSY...

MACK

THE PORCH IS NEITHER INDOORS NOR OUTDOORS.

WHY YOU HERE, RIP VAN WINKLE?

I'M NOT HERE.

I DON'T EXIST.

NEITHER DO YOU.

TEXTBOOK JOSEPH CAMPBELL.

THE WAY CAMPBELL EXPLAINED IT, YOUNG MEN NEED A SECONDARY FATHER TO FINISH RAISING THEM.

BEYOND THEIR BIOLOGICAL FATHER, THEY NEED A SURROGATE, TRADITIONALLY A MINISTER OR A COACH OR A MILITARY OFFICER.

THE FLOTSAM AND JETSAM OF A GENERATION, WASHED UP ON THE BEACH OF LAST RESORT.

THAT'S WHY STREET GANGS ARE SO APPEALING. THEY SEND YOUNG MEN OUT, LIKE KNIGHTS ON QUESTS TO HONE THEIR SKILLS AND PROVE THEMSELVES.

AND ALL THE **TRADITIONAL** MENTORS-- FORGET IT.

MEN ARE PRESUMPTIVE PREDATORS. THEY'RE LEAVING TEACHING IN DROVES.

THE WOULD-BE SPACE MONKEYS WERE WAITING TO GET INSIDE. WHILE SEBASTIAN WAS SCHEMING TO GET HIS SON OUT.

YOU CAN ASSURE MS. CAIN THAT THE DOG IS UNHARMED.

MAYBE WE'RE JUST USING YOUR KID AS BAIT TO GET **YOU** BACK INTO THE GAME?

SO I'M ASLEEP?

IT'S RATHER LIKE YOUR RIGHT AND LEFT BRAINS ARE PLAYING CHESS AGAINST ONE ANOTHER.

IT'S SOMETHING ABOUT MOSES...

VERY GOOD!

YOU CAN READ MY MIND.

MOSES KNEW THAT HE COULDN'T CREATE A SOCIETY OF FREE MEN FROM A GENERATION BORN AS SLAVES.

MOSES KEPT HIS PEOPLE WANDERING UNTIL THE PREVIOUS GENERATION HAD DIED.

YOU'RE NOT HERE.

ANY OF THESE GUYS WOULD KILL FOR THE DESTINY THAT I'M OFFERING YOUR SON.

OUR SON.

JUNIOR HAS TWO DADDIES.

HE'LL PISS IN SOUP AND MAKE SOAP FROM HUMAN FAT, AND BECOME KING OF THE WORLD?

WHAT CAN **YOU** OFFER HIM?

SOME **TRAGIC** LIBERAL ARTS DEGREE?

A MIND-NUMBING CORPORATE JOB?

BUT HE'S JUST A LITTLE BOY.

SO WAS ALEXANDER THE GREAT, ONCE.

HE'LL CHOOSE ME OVER THE WHOLE WORLD...

IF YOU LEAVE TO FIND A BATHROOM--

--OR GET A BEER--

--OR IF YOU GO BUY A BURRITO--

--OR FIND A PLUG-IN FOR YOUR PRECIOUS PHONE--

--DON'T COME BACK!

BUMP

UGH!

CAREFUL.

MY HOME-WORK...

"OPERATION LETHAL INJECTION."

FREE

DON'T...

...GET YOURSELF JABBED.

CULLING THE HERD.

FREE

OR YOU START A CULT.

MY DAD HAS MONEY. I WANT SOMETHING MORE VALUABLE THAN MONEY.

AFTER TWO DECADES IN SCHOOL, NOW I WANT TO LEARN SOMETHING ABOUT MYSELF.

I WANT TO BUILD UP A TREASURE INSIDE OF MYSELF. NOBODY CAN STEAL IT. NO GOVERNMENT CAN EVER TAX IT AWAY.

HERE WAS A FISTFIGHT THERAPY. FOLLOWED BY A GESTALT BOOT CAMP.

PROJECT MAYHEM HAD BEGUN TO PERPETUATE ITS OWN POWER.

YOU OKAY?

RESCUE HIM. HE'LL DESPISE YOU.

I WANT TO HELP.

HE AIN'T HERE TO FIND HIS MOMMY.

MY LIFE'S GOING TO BE OVER BEFORE I KNOW IT. JUST LOOK AT YOU.

THERE'S TOO MANY WAYS TO FEEL GOOD.

CHEER UP. THE NEXT WORLD WILL BE GREAT.

WHAT NEXT WORLD?

BRING YOUR CRAP!

NO MORE. CAPICHE?

I'VE DONE THE DISABILITY THING. I'VE DONE THE MEDICAL MARIJUANA THING. BUT I COULD NEVER GET HIGH ENOUGH TO FORGET THAT I'M ALIVE AND GETTING OLDER...

DELTOIDS ARE, LIKE, THE **CHEEKBONES** OF YOUR WHOLE TORSO!

THE PIECEMEAL ADVICE THAT BOYS INVENT.

WHAT ABOUT YOUR JOB?

HIS JOB.

SIR! MR. DURDEN, SIR!

WE'RE PUTTING YOU THROUGH MED SCHOOL ON THE UNDERSTANDING THAT YOU'D MEET CERTAIN CRITERIA.

MUH-MY G.P.A. IS THREE POINT THREE!

MAKE IT A THREE POINT FIVE.

SIR, THE COURSE WORK THIS TERM--

NEED I REMIND YOU THAT THIS ARRANGEMENT WAS AT YOUR REQUEST?

NO OFFENSE, SIR, BUT RAUL SEYMOUR'S G.P.A. RANKS BELOW MINE.

"MR. SEYMOUR HAS BEEN RELEASED FROM HIS CONTRACT."

GRADUATE IN THE TOP FIVE PERCENT OF YOUR CLASS-- OR MY AGENTS WILL ALSO VOID **YOUR** CONTRACT.

MACK

No, Sebastian's job was never a problem.

Rize or Die International, the world's largest provider of for-hire military personnel.

RIZE OR DIE KEPT THE WORLD SAFE IN SO MANY WAYS.

KNOCK KNOCK

YOU'RE HERE! WHERE'S--?

I MISSED YOU SO MUCH.

BUT... JUNIOR?

WAIT.

AS OUR THIRD COURSE, A SADDLE OF BRAISED VENISON...

A DEAD END.

THE FIRST RULE OF PINT CLUB IS...

NOK·NOK

CASTING IN SESSION

YOU LADIES HERE FOR THE CLUB?

MAYBE.

THE FIRST RULE OF RAW FUCK CLUB IS YOU GO BAREBACK...

FREE

THE FIRST RULE OF FILM CLUB IS YOU DON'T TALK ABOUT ROSEBUD.

FUN FACT--THE REAL-LIFE CLUBS CITED HERE ALL HAVE NAMES INSPIRED BY THE ORIGINAL **FIGHT CLUB**.

BARK

BARK

BARK

BARK

"WE SEE MARLA ENTER..."

BARK

"MARLA ASKS, 'ARE YOU GOD?'"

WHERE'S MY SON?

THIS BORDERS ON BEING TOO META.

BARK

HERE.

BARK

DON'T CALL UNLESS THE PLOT LAGS.

BARK BARK

IS THIS YOUR LITTLE GIRL?

OKAY, MR. CHUCK, WRITE THESE PEOPLE OUT OF OUR SPACE, NOW.

BARK
BARK BARK
BARK
RING RING

JUST FOR A MOMENT.

FREE

RING

Robert Paulson
calling...

YOU FORGET I'M AN OLD LADY.

NO!

YOU! INSIDE!

IT HAD BEEN THREE DAYS.

WE'LL HAVE YOUR MACHINE GUN, TOMORROW.

CAREER ASSIGNMENTS FOR THE FOLLOWING...

SUGARPLUM? SOMALIA?

INTO THE HEART OF DARKNESS.

RWANDA?

STRAIGHT TO THE BELLY OF THE BEAST.

MONKEY MARSHALL--

YOUR MARCHING ORDERS!

Marshall

AN *ISIS* SUICIDE BOMBER!

BEATS SOAP DUTY.

YOU'RE *SO* LUCKY!

ANGOLA-- SERIOUSLY?

DON'T FORGET MY AK-47.

YOU GOING TO FIGHT CLUB?

TONIGHT?

RUNNING WOLF THOUGHT HE COULD JUST PICK UP WHERE HE LEFT OFF.

WE CHECK I.D.

THE FIRST RULE OF FIGHT CLUB...

EVERYTHING WAS THE SAME.

EXCEPT RUNNING WOLF.

SIZING UP THE TALENT. LOOKING FOR SOME MAN MORE OR LESS JUST LIKE HIMSELF.

YOU WANT A FIGHT?

PICK ON SOMEBODY YOUR OWN AGE.

LIKE, MAYBE, ABRAHAM LINCOLN.

YOU GOT A FIGHT YET?

STILL LOOKING.

PUT US ON THE LIST.

YOU AND ME?

HA HAAH HAA!

SORRY, GRAMPS.

HA HAA!

NO DISRESPECT, MISTER, BUT YOU'D BE LIKE FIGHTING MY CRIPPLED PAW-PAW.

DOESN'T EVERY SON WANT TO FIGHT HIS OLD MAN?

MISTER, GO HOME.

BUZZ

BUZZ

Calling...

MARLA

SEBASTIAN?

BOOM

CHOOM

BLAM BLAM BLAM BLAM

MOGADISHU! THE BOKO HARAM ARE SHELLING OUR POSITION.

SNAP

GET HUMAN SACRIFICE NUMBER 2388. HE'LL BE A DOCTOR BY NOW...

YOU!

ORDERS SPECIFIED-- "NOT THE FACE!"

WHO'S HE NOW?

MR. DURDEN, DUH.

IT'S LIKE WORKING FOR STEVE JOBS.

SCRAPE

I MAKE NO APOLOGIES FOR MY CARBON FOOTPRINT.

BOOM

BLAM BLAM

RATATATA

YOU'RE SHIVERING.

KAFF. GASP KAFF.

JUST OLD AGE, DEAR.

I WISH I COULD GIVE YOU A FEW YEARS OF MY LIFE.

IN CASE WE DIE, I HAVE A CONFESSION.

RATA TATA TAT

WHAT IS IT, HONEY? DID YOU STEAL A CANDY BAR?

BLAM BLAM

I'M NOT ELEVEN YEARS OLD.

YOU'RE YOUNGER?

I'M LIKE YOU!

HOW?

OLD AND DECREPIT!

BOOM

WHAT DID I HAVE TO LOSE?

HOW OLD?

I'M INCAPABLE OF GIVING LOVE!

HOW OLD?!

BOOOM

NO ONE CARES ABOUT A DYING ADULT. BUT A DYING CHILD...

HOW OLD?

DECADES AGO, I WENT TO CANCER GROUPS--

CHOOM

--I DIDN'T HAVE CANCER, BUT IT MADE ME FEEL SO GOOD.

ARE YOU GASLIGHTING ME?

THE MORE I FOOL PEOPLE INTO LOVING ME...THE MORE I HATE MYSELF.

I NEED A CIGARETTE.

STAY ON TASK, TRACY.

SUPPORT GROUPS BRING ME LOVE I'M NOT OBLIGED TO RECIPROCATE.

BOOM
BOOM
BOOM

SECONDHAND SMOKE KILLS.

THEY'RE NOT ALONE.

CRICK

DON'T CRY.

IT'S THE TEAR GAS.

WHAT DO YOU SEE?

THIS TREASURE REPRESENTED EVERY BOLD IDEA.

EVERY DROP OF HUMAN SWEAT. DISTILLED DOWN TO THESE PRECIOUS ITEMS.

YOU'VE COME BACK!

COFFEY'S DOG. NOT BURNED ALIVE.

WELCOME BACK, SIR!

THIS NUMBER IS NO LONGER IN SERVICE.

...NO LONGER IN SERVICE.

WHAT'S THIS?

When I Was A
Boy, What Did
I Most Dream
Of Becoming?
(Be Honest)

A. A Priest

B. God

(If You Chose
Any Answer
Other Than "B"
We Encourage
You To Seek
Employment
Elsewhere.)

Complete
The Following
Statement:

"WAR IS..."

A. Unhealthy For
Children and
Animals and
Other Living
Creatures

B. Immensely
Profitable

ANSWER THE QUESTIONS. DON'T ASK THEM.

The Highest
Form of
Authority
Resides In:

A. Tyler Durden

B. Tyler Durden

HE COULD STILL SMELL CHOCOLATE FROM THE DREAM.

Complete
The Following
Statement:

"THE WORLD IS..."

A. Our Mother

B. My Oyster

IF THE S.A.T.'S WERE TOUGH...

FAIL THIS AND YOU DIE.

THEY COME SHOOT ME?

NO, BUT YOU'LL BE JUST AS DEAD.

GNARLY-ASSED BRUISE, OLD MAN.

IT WASN'T A BRUISE.

IT WASN'T A DREAM.

IT WAS CHOCOLATE.

MY SON KISSED ME.

MY KID'S NEVER KISSED ME, NOT SPONTANEOUSLY...

MY WIFE LUSTS AFTER ME... MY SON LOVES ME... BUT ONLY WHEN I'M NOT MYSELF...

POOR SEBASTIAN.

≥SIGH≤

IT'S TIME FOR HIM TO DIE.

OPEN YOUR TRAP.

HOMEWORK ASSIGNMENT.

THE FIRST RULE IS YOU HAVE TO SWALLOW.

BOTTOMS UP.

≡GULP≡

FEEDING TIME.

WHAT AM I TAKING?

RAT POISON.

RAT POISON!

WARFARIN.

ANTICOAGULANT.

BLOOD THINNER.

IN 1974, A VANDAL...

"IN 1914...

"REMBRANDT'S *THE NIGHT WATCH*, IN 1911...

"AND IN 1975...

"LET'S NOT FORGET 1990..."

EVEN THE MONA LISA...

1956.

ALSO 1956. A BAD YEAR.

1974.

2009.

FUN FACT: YES. A DILDO.

HERE'S THE BEST SPOT.

PSEUDO-EPHEDRINE.

VASOCONSTRICTOR.

ONE RAZOR BLADE, EACH.

I'M NOT SLASHING ANY PAINTING.

GENTLEMEN, THE MEDIAN CUBITAL VEIN.

PROJECT HOSE DOWN.

"USE YOUR ARM LIKE A PUMP-ACTION SHOTGUN."

SQUEEZE IT TO SHOOT FARTHER.

144

EACH STAKE OUT A DIFFERENT PICTURE.

WAIT FOR MY SIGNAL.

WHAT SIGNAL?

PULL DOWN

A BOMB TO EXPLODE ALL THE WORTHLESS FURNITURE INSIDE SEBASTIAN'S HEAD...

ESTÁ MUERTO.

VITAMIN K.

BUT TYLER.

I ANSWER TO A HIGHER POWER THAN MR. DURDEN.

UNHAPPY MARRIAGE.

"YOU KNOW WHAT A HOLLYWOOD SQUIB IS?

THIS SIDE OUT

"NO ONE COULD KNOW IT WAS A JERRY-RIGGED CLUMP OF ELBOW MACARONI GLUED TO SOME MONKEY FUR."

NOT ALL HEADSHOTS ARE FATAL.

SOME HEADSHOTS...

"...AREN'T EVEN HEAD-SHOTS."

BUT WHY?

TO GREEN-LIGHT ALL OF HIS SOCIAL PROGRAMS.

A GREAT SOCIETY... A WAR ON POVERTY...

"MAKING FATHERS A HANDICAP IN MILLIONS OF HOUSEHOLDS..."

THAT'S CONSPIRACY THEORY BULLSHIT...

LET'S END THIS BULLSHIT.

TWO HUNDRED VALIUMS OUGHT TO DO THE TRICK.

COMMIT MURDER?

WE HAVE A CONTRACT.

NO DISRESPECT, MR. DURDEN...

TICK

YOUR FORTY-FIVE MINUTES ARE UP.

TOCK

SNAP

WHAT WENT ON?

HE LOOKS FAMILIAR, BUT I WANT TO SAY HIS NAME WAS...RUNNING WOLF?

IT WAS.

THE RUNNING WOLF I KNEW HAD CANCER. I'M SURE HE'S DEAD.

RIZE OR DIE... SOUNDS LIKE A SUPPORT GROUP.

I TRIED TO SEDUCE HIM.

DID YOU HAVE HANDCUFFS? PORNO MOVIES?

HOW DID--?

WHAT'S YOUR NAME?

MYRTLE? HAZEL? AFTER LYING SO LONG I CAN'T REMEMBER.

I GOT IT!

YOU DIDN'T DIE!

NO, I STARTED DATING A GUY IN MY SICKLE CELL ANEMIA GROUP. AREN'T BLACK MEN WONDERFUL!

HOW ARE YOU?

I HAVE A FOR-REAL MALIGNANCY. BUT I'VE BEEN FAKE DYING FOR SO LONG THAT REAL DEATH FEELS LIKE A RELIEF.

I KNOW! LET'S CELEBRATE!

Magic Wand
FOUNDATION

Conta

I NEED YOU TO AIRDROP A TOASTED CHEESE SANDWICH AT THE FOLLOWING G.P.S. COORDINATES...

HUNGRY?

A PIÑA COLADA.

AND A JET, FUELED AND READY, WAITING IN DAKAR.

AND LOTS OF PIÑA COLADAS!

YOUR SON IS IN OUR PROTECTION.

UNTIL I FALL ASLEEP.

BUZZ

SELL PEOPLE SOMETHING THEY CAN USE ONLY ONCE. SOAP AND BOMBS FIT THE BILL, PERFECTLY.

BUZZ

GIVE A NOBLE REASON FOR MURDER. HITLER UNDERSTOOD THAT.

BUZZ

MARLA?

YOU'RE SUCH A TOOL.

WHO--?

DOC HEADSHRINKER DECEIVED YOU FOR TEN YEARS. NOW YOU BELIEVE HIM?

WHO IS IT?

IT'S YOUR DISEASED SUBCONSCIOUS.

OUR GOOD DOCTOR IS LEADING YOU TO SLAUGHTER.

HANG UP. NOW.

HE'LL BUTCHER YOUR SON.

TYLER DURDEN PLANS TO KILL YOU.

WHY?

FOR THE SAME REASON HE KILLED YOUR PARENTS.

YOU KILLED MY MOM AND DAD?

HE'S CRAZY AMBITIOUS! WHY ELSE WOULD HE BE COMPLICIT WITH EVERYTHING I'VE DONE?

FOR A DECADE, I'VE BEEN STUDYING YOUR CASE. TO CURE YOU.

TYLER KNOWS THAT KILLING ME WOULD BE SUICIDE.

YOUR DISORDER, IT'S CONGENITAL.

INHERITED?

IT DIDN'T MANIFEST AS FULL BLOWN UNTIL YOUR PARENTS WERE GONE.

MI PADRE ES SU PADRE.

TYLER WON'T DIE. HE'S ALREADY INSINUATED HIMSELF IN YOUR SON'S LIFE.

HOW DO YOU THINK YOUR SON MADE THE INCENDIARY BOMB TO DESTROY YOUR HOUSE?

LISTEN TO ME!

SO, TYLER IS SOME SORT OF CONTAGION?

HE'S AN **ARCHETYPE.** TYLER WORKS LIKE A SUPERSTITION OR A PREJUDICE. HE BECOMES PART OF THE LENS THROUGH WHICH YOU SEE THE WORLD.

MORE BLACK-HELICOPTER BULLSHIT.

TAPED TO THE BOTTOM OF YOUR SEAT...

DO YOU KNOW SHE'S DEAD?

A DRONE FOUND...

TYLER SURVIVES ACROSS TIME BY INFECTING ONE GENERATION AFTER ANOTHER.

DOC GUTLESS THINKS I'M A BULLSHIT *MEME*?

DON'T YOU CARE?

SHOOT HIM!

DON'T EVEN CONSIDER SHOOTING ME.

WITHOUT MY GUIDANCE, YOU'LL BECOME A RAVING LUNATIC.

WE ARE, EACH OF US, IDEAS THAT FIGHT FOR OUR OWN SURVIVAL.

"UNLESS YOU CAN DEFEAT HIM...

"...TYLER WILL WIPE OUT EVERY HUMAN WHO DOESN'T WORSHIP HIM LIKE A GOD."

I SAID NO TO A LOT OF GUYS BEFORE I SAID YES TO SEBASTIAN.

SMARTER GUYS. RICH ONES.

WHY SEBASTIAN?

I DON'T KNOW.

A PERSON CAN'T DIE AS LONG AS I'VE BEEN DYING AND NOT MAKE A FEW FRIENDS.

RING

RING

RING

TALK TO ME.

ANGELA HERE, FROM ASCENDING BOWEL CANCERS.

05-09-15 SAT
21:27:03   27

STREET SURVEILLANCE VIDEO SHOWS THE BOY BOARDING THE NUMBER 17 BUS.

WHO WAS WITH HIM?

TOMAS HERE-- FROM METASTASIZED MELANOMAS--THE KID IS SOLO.

05-09-15   SAT

HE TRANSFERRED TO THE NUMBER 45.

22:12:45:03

DOES HE HAVE A HISTORY OF SOMNAMBULISM?

HE WASN'T KIDNAPPED?

DEVEN HERE-- PARASITICAL BRAIN INFECTIONS--FACIAL RECOGNITION PUTS HIM AT THE AIRPORT.

0021-5656-VT

AT 3:32 A.M.

DEPARTED U.S. AIRSPACE AT OH EIGHT HUNDRED HOURS GREENWICH MEAN.

AND SWITCHED OFF ITS TRANSPONDER.

WAS THERE SOMEONE NEW IN YOUR CHILD'S LIFE? A STRANGER?

...HOW MUCH POTASSIUM NITRATE DO I ADD?

...WHAT ABOUT THE POWDERED MANGANESE?

SWEETHEART, WHO'S ON THE PHONE?

NOBODY.

THERE WAS NOBODY.

171

SECOND CORPORAL JENNINGS. RUTGERS. TOP TEN PERCENT.

NICE GRADES, JENNINGS!

THANKS FOR PUTTING A GUN TO MY HEAD, SIR!

WHAT YOU FAIL TO GRASP IS THAT TYLER DURDEN BROUGHT MARLA SINGER INTO YOUR HOME.

HE **BRED** THE TWO OF YOU LIKE FARM ANIMALS.

TO CREATE A VEHICLE FOR HIMSELF.

MY POINT IS...

HUMAN BEINGS DON'T CULTIVATE IDEAS.

ON THE CONTRARY...

MACK

SIGN HERE.

GOT A FORKLIFT?

I'LL CALL HIM.

DON'T!

CALLING HIM AIN'T CONTROLLING HIM.

HIS NAME IS ROBERT PAULSON!

BOOM

BOOM

UNLOAD CRATES.

JCLEAR
VARHEAD
FRAGILE

IDEAS ARE PARASITES.

CAREFUL, HE'S ARMED.

HAVE YOU READ THE SORROWS OF YOUNG WERTHER? PUBLISHED IN 1774?

TOSS YOUR WEAPON OUT THE WINDOW!

THERE'S A GLOCK THIRTY-NINE--FORTY-FIVE G.A.P. IN THE MINI-BAR...A GERBER FIXED-BLADE COMBAT KNIFE STASHED UNDER THE FLOOR MAT...

THE NOVEL DEPICTS A YOUNG MAN IN LOVE WITH A MARRIED WOMAN.

THROUGHOUT EUROPE PEOPLE CALLED IT "WERTHER FEVER." WEARING YELLOW PANTS AND BLUE JACKETS...

Crack!

MUCH OF THAT GENERATION ALSO KILLED THEMSELVES.

KILL HIM.

CENTURIES LATER, WHEN A SUICIDE SPURS COPYCATS, PSYCHOLOGISTS STILL CALL IT THE "WERTHER EFFECT."

HERE LIES METT WELSH 866-1888

HAROLD MILFORD 1799-1822

REST IN PEACE OUR DARLING SON LLEWELLYN BOYCE 1801

CHRISTOPHER SMALLWOOD 1845-1864

JEREMY WALLIS Beloved Son 1838-1859

MY POINT IS THAT FICTIONAL CHARACTERS CAN SURVIVE THEIR READERS.

THE FIRST RULE OF FIGHT CLUB IS...

TYLER? DID YOU CO-OPT MY KID?

WHAT'S A DELAYED-IGNITION FUSE...?

NO PARAFFIN. GOT IT.

HOW LONG FOR THE TIMER?

WHAT? ARE YOU...**CHARLIE BROWN?**

I'M HERE BECAUSE YOU NEEDED ME.

YOU REMEMBER THE FIGHTS.

WAR ON TELEVISION WAS EVERY BEDTIME STORY.

"FIGHTING IN THE MIDDLE EAST AND TERRORIST BOMBINGS IN NORTHERN IRELAND. VIETNAM. QUEBEC. GRENADA. IRAN. IRAQ. AFGHANISTAN. BASQUE SEPARATISTS.

TING INTENSIFIES...REBEL IN

"DOMESTIC TERROR. SCHOOL SHOOTINGS. ANTHRAX.

"BUT THE MORE WE DEMANDED STRAWBERRY FIELDS, FOREVER..."

DIVORCE DIDN'T RESOLVE ANYTHING.

HE WOULDN'T *SN*BARKBARKBARK BY IF YOU SPENT QU BARK BARK WITH HIM INSTEAD *XX*BARK BARK WHORES!

HE'S SUCH A N*BARKBARK* BECAUSE YOU'RE A CA BARKTING G BARK BARK

"I JUST STEPPED IN AS PEACEMAKER."

NOW WE'LL BRING PEACE TO THE ENTIRE WORLD.

WHAT'S TODAY?

I SHOULDN'T.

BZZT BZZT

IT'S THURSDAY.

THE DAY OF THE MONTH?

TO REACH THE KID, WHY NOT JUST CALL HIM?

ARE YOU...?

MAYBE. PROBABLY.

HER KID HAS A PHONE.

RUNNING WOLF WILL BE **THRILLED!**

IT'S NOT HIS.

FIND A LISTING FOR TYLER DURDEN.

WAP

IT'S MR. DURDEN FOR YOU, SIR.

REALLY?! MY DAD'S COMING HERE?

WHY WOULD HE PRETEND TO BE YOU?

HOLD ON. I HAVE ANOTHER CALL.

BABY?

MOM?

BABY, WHERE ARE YOU?

DAD'S COMING.

WHAT DOES **DENOUNCE** MEAN?

CONSENT CREATES A **GAME**, NOT A CRIME.

"MUTUAL CONSENT."

WITH RIZE OR DIE, EVERY BATTLE IS CONSENSUAL, RENDERING IT, IN EFFECT-- **PLAY**...

"WAR HAS BECOME A CONTINUOUS SPORTING EVENT.

"A WORLD CUP THAT NEVER ENDS."

MODERN WAR IS MERELY MEDIA CONTENT.

INSTEAD OF LIVING THEIR LIVES AS COGS IN SOME IMPERSONAL MACHINE, WE GIVE PEOPLE A MEANS TO FEEL **ALIVE.**

OR THEY'LL DIE.

MEN DIE EVERY DAY, COMMUTING TO SOUL-KILLING JOBS.

Ideas
Breed
Us

MACK

LET'S GET THIS STRAIGHT... TYLER IS SOME INFECTIOUS MENTAL VIRUS?

WE GET IT.

THEN HOW CAN YOU RESOLVE HIM?

WUMP

I CAN'T.

TRY REMOVING SANTA CLAUS FROM THE CULTURAL LANDSCAPE.

RING RING

THAT'S CHLOE. HOW CAN I TELL HER THEY'RE ALL DOOMED?

RING RING

I THOUGHT WE AGREED NO PHONES.

"WE SEE THE EXTERIOR OF THE MAGIC WAND FOUNDATION..."

CHLOE, SIX MORE 747'S ARE ALREADY ROUTED TO YOUR COORDINATES.

RING RING

BEEP

WE'VE ALREADY LANDED A DOZEN FLIGHTS.

FOR A TOTAL OF 7,345 MEDICALLY FRAGILE CHILDREN.

THERE'S NOTHING THERE.

ANOTHER FIVE THOUSAND KIDS WANT PASSAGE TO THAT SPOT.

AND THEY ALL WANT AK-47'S.

SAY IT'S A SUMMER CAMP.

FORGET ANY TRAFFIC JAM. HALF THE BIRDS AREN'T LANDING.

...SKYDIVING LESSONS?

STALKING PANTHER TO REVENGING EAGLE...

I COPY. GIVE ME SIXTY SECONDS.

59 SECONDS

55 SECOND

KNOCK-KNOCK

CAN JUNIOR COME OUT TO PLAY?

BEAT IT, OLD MAN.

DO YOU KNOW WHAT TIME IT IS?

IT'S 3:45.

9 SECON

4 SECOND

IT'S TIME TO DIE A HERO'S DEATH.

BOOOM

REVENGING EAGLE, DO YOU COPY? COME IN, REVENGING EAGLE!

OH, TIMMY...

SIGNAL LOST

DRAGON SQUAD, DO YOU COPY?

DRAGON SQUAD, COMMENCE **OPERATION INFERNO!**

FWOOSH

BZZ BZZ

JUNIOR
Calling

PUMPKIN...

WHO IS THIS?

YOUR SON WAS JUST OUR LURE.

WE'RE SAVING THOUSANDS OF SPECIES.

I WANTED TO SAVE YOU, TOO.

SQUEEE MEOW MEOW WHINNY M. OYNK TWEET GRRR NEIGH MOOO OYNK MOOOO GRRR SNORT

THESE ARE THE LABS WHERE WE BREWED UP BUBONIC PLAGUE, THE SPANISH INFLUENZA, A.I.D.S., EBOLA, BUT NONE OF THEM GAVE US THE UNIVERSAL MORTALITY RATE WE NEEDED.

NEIGH MEOW SNORT SNORT GRR OYNK

MORTALITY RATES?

SQUEE MOOO

IN THESE SAME LABS, WE NOW PRESERVE LIFE.

NOAH'S STRATEGY WASN'T EVEN REMOTELY REALISTIC.

BUT WHY?

DON'T PLAY COY WITH ME.

IN ELEVEN SECONDS, EIGHTEEN MINUTES, AND ZERO HOURS, WE'RE RE-BOOTING CIVILIZATION.

THIS MAN IS THE FIRST DIRECTOR OF PROTOCOL. HIS NAME IS WILKINS. NO ONE ON STAFF MAY ADDRESS TYLER DURDEN DIRECTLY UNTIL WILKINS HAS BID YOU A FORMAL WELCOME. THE SECOND SECRETARY OF STRATEGIC OPERATIONS WILL NOW TAKE YOUR COAT...

HOW DO I TELL MY SON THAT HIS MOTHER IS DEAD?

AS FIRST DIRECTOR OF PROTOCOL, I BID YOU WELCOME, MR. DURDEN.

KAH-BLOOM

WHERE'S THE BOY?

BUZZ BUZZ

BUZZ

TYLER DURDEN Calling...

TYLER HERE.

YOU'RE ONLY FOOLING YOURSELF.

BIG DADDY NEEDS A TIME-OUT.

WHAT NOW?

MR. DURDEN?

217

FIFTEEN MINUTES REMAINING.

WE REALLY MUST SHELTER BELOW-GROUND, SIR.

I DIDN'T TELL YOU SOMETHING.

WHEN YOU MET RUNNING WOLF...

NOW, EXPERIENCE YOUR ROOT CHAKRA BLOSSOMING...

"I CAN'T RECIPROCATE LOVE. IT'S NO SURPRISE THAT I ENDED UP WITH HAMISH."

"MARLA, DON'T YOU MEAN RUNNING WOLF?"

"WHATEVER."

WHAT WE HAVE IS LESS LOVE THAN IT IS A SHARED EMOTIONAL DISABILITY.

WHAT ARE YOU SAYING?

I'M A LOUSY MOTHER.

YOU'RE PUTTING YOUR BUTT ON THE LINE.

WHY?

WHY WHAT?

WHY MOGADISHU, CHLOE?

WHY SEND KIDS TO ALL THOSE HELLHOLES?

I CALLED FOR PLOT ADVICE.

THE WRITER WITH THE WRETCHED NAME.

Poloni

End Call

RING RING

YIKES, THEY'RE CALLING FOR PLOT ADVICE!

DON'T PICK UP!

RING RING

GEEZ, GUYS, YOU CAN'T NOT PICK UP!

SOME ZOMBIES, RIGHT HERE, WOULD IMPROVE THIS IMMENSELY...

WHY CAN'T YOU BE NICE AND JUST TELL THEM?

RING RING

AND THE MICHELANGELOS?

MR. DURDEN, SIR!

DADDY!

...I AM TYLER.

I WANT YOU TO HIT ME AS HARD AS YOU CAN, DADDY...

NO.

DOESN'T EVERY SON WANT TO FIGHT HIS OLD MAN?

HE'S ALWAYS HIGH ON PILLS, BUT HE'S STILL MY DADDY!

NNGH!

SEEMS LIKE OLD TIMES.

JUNIOR!

RUNNING WOLF?

YOU'RE ALIVE...

WAK

AS HARD AS YOU CAN...

TYLER! WHY CHOOSE SUCH **WORTHLESS** PEOPLE?

MR. DURDEN, OCCUPY ME!

MAKE **ME** YOUR VESSEL!

∹GASP∻

?

WHAT'S THE TRANQUILITY GAME...

NORSE MYTHOLOGY...

DAY		HOURS		MINUTES		SECONDS
00		00	:	08	:	11

EVERY SOCIETY HAS ITS CLEANSING MYTH.

"...RAGNAROK CALLS FOR THE ELITE CLASS TO HIDE WHILE THE REST OF THE WORLD HUNTS ONE ANOTHER TO EXTINCTION."

LIKEWISE, THE MASQUE OF THE RED DEATH.

EVEN HELTER SKELTER CALLED FOR MANSON TO HIDE IN A DEEP, DESERT BURROW WHILE RACE WARS WOULD DECIMATE MANKIND.

GENESIS, CHAPTER SIX, VERSES ELEVEN THROUGH FIFTEEN.

...FOR TOO LONG, WEAKNESS HAS BEEN REWARDED...

...YOUR LABORS WERE SIPHONED AWAY FOR THE BENEFIT OF COMPLAINERS...

WHAT'S HAPPENING?

...THESE CAVERNS WILL SERVE THE WOMB...

WE R AS THE IS S CLE

AS OUR AGENTS TRIGGER NUCLEAR BLASTS AROUND GLOBE...

BOOM

RUMMM

BBBLL

BARK

BARK

WE'RE IN THE BOTTOM OF AN HOURGLASS.

KAH-RASH

BOOMM

GETTING BURIED ALIVE.

DADDY, ARE WE GOING TO DIE?

DOES ANYBODY HAVE A XANAX?

YOU WANT A VICODIN?

I'LL TRADE XANAX FOR AMBIEN.

CAN I CALL YOU BACK?

KILLING THE DOG WOULD GIVE YOU GREATER AUTHORITY.

CAN HE GET TO THE STAGE?

THE STAGE?

YOU WILL BREED ONLY PERFECT ANIMALS...

WE HAVE PRESER[V]... THAT IS YOUR INH[E]... AS OUR AGENTS TR[...] YOU WILL BREED O[N]... [HIS]TORY IS DEAD... [THE] DEAD ARE D[E]... [WE] HAVE DONE... [WE] MUST REST... [WE] MUST MOUR[N]... [WE] MUST DEDIC... [THE] END OF AL[L]...

RRRMBBL[L]

BOOM

WHERE ARE YOU GOING?

HE'S PERSEUS PETITIONING THE GODS.

I LIKE BEING A GOD.

YOU'VE BEEN BEATEN BY YOUR WIFE, YOUR NEIGHBOR, BY THE RELIC...EVEN BY YOUR SON.

YOU WILL NOT BE BEATEN BACK NOW.

KRASH

RECITE THE REST.

HISTORY--

BOOM

HISTORY IS D[EAD]

247

...HISTORY IS DEAD...

BOOMMM

HOLD UP THE PHONE.

THE DEAD ARE DEAD...

KAH-

Polonic

-BOOM

RRMMRL

THE SCRIPT.

CRASH

I FORGET.

Polonic

TYLER KNEW IT.

KBOOM

"...HAPPILY EVER AFTER!"

WHAT?

THEY DIE? ALL THE MAGIC WAND DO-GOODERS, AND THE SICK CHILDREN-- EVEN **CHLOE?**

SOME WARMED-OVER **ATLAS SHRUGGED** REDUX?

AND WE'RE ALL BURNED TO CINDERS AND SHIT?

DO WE LOOK BURNED?

AM I MISSING SOMETHING?

WELL PLAYED, PALAHNIUK...

AM I CORRECT IN ASSUMING IT'S THE BAD GUYS WHO'LL DIE?

THE WAY THE CATHOLIC CHURCH SLAUGHTERED THE CATHARS?

HOW MANY CATHARS DO YOU SEE THESE DAYS?

OKAY, MR. SMUG, WHAT ABOUT THE EXPLOSIONS?

DRAGON SQUAD-- DETONATE OBJECTIVE!

THE ONLY WAY TO RESOLVE TYLER WAS TO IDENTIFY AND EXECUTE ALL HIS ACOLYTES.

THIS RUNS SMACK INTO **DEUS EX MACHINA** TERRITORY.

I STILL DON'T GET IT.

DUMMY NUKES...

'TH CARE
ARHEAD

HANDLE WITH CARE
NUCLEAR WARHEAD

NOT FOR
RETAIL SALE

amazzon

CUT OFF THE HEAD!

"...DID IT SEEM A LITTLE TOO EASY THAT ONE CRAZY MAN COULD CONTROL THE WORLD?"

THE TESTS. THEY WERE BAIT.

SHE MEANS LIKE A ROACH MOTEL.

GENOCIDAL NEO-FASCISTS CHECK IN, BUT THEY DON'T CHECK OUT.

I TRICKED THE TRICKSTER.

YOU'RE JEALOUS. PEOPLE LIKED TYLER TOO MUCH.

PREPARE FOR READER BACKLASH.

DING-DONG

BARK BARK BARK

NOT TO MENTION THAT AFTER ALL THAT...

"...YOU KILLED THE DOG."

CHUCK, YOU CLIMAXED PREMATURELY.

CUT.

YOU JUST GAVE UP.

PRINT!

SHUT UP AND LISTEN!

THE END!

CLEVER YOU.

BARK BARK BARK

BARK BARK

YOU GUYS?

FINI.

BE MISERABLE.

LIDIA'S RIGHT.

THAT I'M MISERABLE?

NO. THIS IS NOT THE END.

BARK BARK BARK

BARK BARK

BARK BARK BARK BARK BARK

HEY.

HEY.

May I never be perfect and complete

The things you own end up owning you

FUCK
who you
want to
FUCK

cough

IF YOU WANT NEIL GAIMAN, I COULD DRAW YOU A MAP.

WE'RE LOOKING FOR YOU.

LET'S HANDLE THIS VIA REDDIT--

THIS ENDING SUCKS.

SO DOES LIFE.

THAT'S WHY WE LIKE TYLER.

HE'S A SOCIOPATHIC KILLING MACHINE...

BUT IN HIS NIHILISTIC WAY, TYLER IS A BIG-TIME OPTIMIST.

IN THE BOOK, THE ENDING WAS DIFFERENT.

YOU DON'T EVEN **HAVE** BOWEL CANCER!

YOU DON'T HAVE BOWEL CANCER EITHER!

HE'S NOT EVEN A NAVAJO!

WHEN THEY WERE ON THE ROOF...

SEBASTIAN DECEIVED HIS COMMUNITY INTO LOVING HIM. THAT WAY HE DIDN'T HAVE TO RECIPROCATE THEIR LOVE.

IN FACT, HE DESPISED THEM FOR LOVING HIM BECAUSE ONLY IDIOTS WOULD LOVE SOMETHING SO REPREHENSIBLE...

WAIT-- THERE **WAS** A BOOK?

YES, YOU CHUCKLEHEADS!

VICTIMS FORGIVE THEIR VICTIMIZER. THAT'S THE REDEMPTION.

WHAT'S NEXT, CHIEF?

FOR STARTERS, WE CAN FORGIVE CHUCK FOR THE INCREDIBLY LAME ENDING HE'D PLANNED.

AFTER THAT, LET'S GO CREATE THE ENDING WE WANT.

♪♪♪ ♪♪♪♪ ♪♪♪

I VOTE THAT...

...THEN, IT COULD...

♪♪♪♪ ♪♪♪ ♪ ♪♪♪

WHO WON THE SCRATCH-AND-SNIFF CONTEST?

AGREED.

WHERE--?

WE WANT TO SURPRISE YOU.

YOU CAN'T. I'M **WRITING** THIS.

YOU CAN'T TEACH GOD ANYTHING.

DON'T USE MY TRUISMS AGAINST ME!

LET ME WRITE US A FLEET OF JETS.

QUIT CONTROLLING.

BETTER WEATHER?

STOP IT.

STOP WHAT?

BEING CLEVER.

THAT'S CAMERON STEWART, NOT ME.

ARE WE THERE YET?

I REFUSE TO GIVE READERS AN UPLIFTING FAUX EXPERIENCE ENGINEERED TO COMFORT THEM AND PERPETUATE THE SOCIOPOLITICAL AND ECONOMIC STATUS QUO.

WHO DIED AND MADE YOU BERTOLT BRECHT?

HOLD UP.

NNNG!

MMF!

HIS NAME WAS ROBERT PAULSON.

HIS NAME WAS ROBERT PAULSON.

HIS NAME WAS ROBERT PAULSON.

!

CRACK

CRUNCH

SNAP

POP

GRIND

BARK
BARK

BARK

TYLER
ABANDONED
US.

I TRIED TO
SEDUCE HIM
INTO COMING
BACK.

I APPRECIATE THE GESTURE, BUT--SORRY-- I'M STILL ME.

I LIKED MY GENOCIDAL ENDING...

NO ONE ELSE CAN SEE ME.

FUCK who you want to FUCK

I CAN.

DON'T SCOTCH THIS.

SUBTLE. FIRST YOU END ON THE WORLD'S TALLEST BUILDING. THIS ENDS UNDER-GROUND?

SHE'S A PISTOL.

MY CHARACTER IS HITTING ON MY FRIENDS?

WRITE LIDIA AND ME A SEX SCENE.

YOU'RE GETTING US SUED.

DON'T YOU WANT RESOLUTION?

I KNOW THE END...!

"...EVERYONE GOES BACK TO WANDERING...

"...A FEW PEOPLE WANDER AWAY."

HAPPY ANNIVERSARY.

GUYS?

THIS APP SHOWS PEOPLE AROUND THE WORLD STILL BURIED ALIVE!

I VOTE WE GO SAVE THEM!

LET'S GO FORGIVE THEM!

SOUNDS REDEMPTIVE E...

HIP-HIP HU...

DA VINCI USED TO TELL ME--

LEONARDO DA VINCI?

HE SAID, "ART IS NEVER FINISHED, ABANDO--

YOU'RE CALLING THIS ART?

WHY CAN'T OUR HAPPY ENDING INCLUDE CHUCK?

THIS IS CHUCK'S HAPPY ENDING.

WE MAKE OUR LIVES INTO STORIES--AND STORIES INTO OUR LIVES.

OKAY, NOW YOU'RE SELF-ISOLATING **AND** YOU'RE BABBLING.

IT'S NOT ENOUGH TO TRANSFORM YOUR CHARACTER.

A GOO STORY SH ALSO SU AND TRAN THE AUTHO THE READ

THIS MAKES IT A HAPPY ENDING.

WHAT'S NEXT, CHIEF?

Wo... Health Center

A woman can never be TOO RICH, TOO THIN, or TOO CLOSE TO THE EDGE of THE TABLE

IT'S NOT MY HUSBAND'S.

DA-DA!

YOU FORGET THE BIG LINE.

WHAT LINE?

IT GOT CUT FROM THE FILM.

SOMEDAY, I WANT TO HAVE YOUR ABORTION.

JUST A LITTLE SOMETHING WE IN THE WRITING BIZ LIKE TO CALL A PAY-OFF.

YOU WRITTEN THE CLINIC PART YET?

NO, NOT YET.

Chuck Palahniuk, writer

CHUCK PALAHNIUK is the author of fourteen novels—*Beautiful You, Doomed, Damned, Tell-All, Pygmy, Snuff, Rant, Haunted, Diary, Lullaby, Choke, Invisible Monsters, Survivor,* and *Fight Club*—which all have sold more than five million copies in the United States. He is also the author of *Fugitives and Refugees*, published as part of the Crown Journeys series; the nonfiction collection *Stranger Than Fiction*; and the short story collection *Make Something Up*. He lives in the Pacific Northwest. Visit him on the web at ChuckPalahniuk.net.

Cameron Stewart, interior artist

CAMERON STEWART is an award-winning writer and artist of comics, including *B.P.R.D. Hell on Earth: Exorcism, Batgirl, Batman and Robin, Assassin's Creed,* and many more. He has won Eisner and Shuster Awards and been nominated for Harvey, Eagle, and Bram Stoker Awards for his original graphic novel *Sin Titulo*. Originally from Toronto, he has also lived and worked in Montreal, Berlin, London, and Glasgow. He punched someone once. It didn't work out so well.

David Mack, cover artist

DAVID MACK is the *New York Times* best-selling author and artist of the *Kabuki* series and the writer and artist of *Daredevil* from Marvel Comics. Mack created artwork for the opening titles of the *Jessica Jones* Netflix TV series. For the number-one hit film *Captain America: The Winter Soldier*, Mack worked with Sarofsky Design to create the art and concept for the credit and title sequence. Mack's work has garnered nominations for seven Eisner Awards, four International Eagle Awards, and both the Harvey and Kirby Awards in the category of Best New Talent, as well as many other national and international awards.

Dave Stewart, colorist

DAVE STEWART was born on the high desert while his mother danced to the chatter of a rattlesnake's tail. Despite a rare case of Sasquatch leg and the desire to run with any northbound moose migration, he found the coloring arts were a suitable profession to fuel the resources needed to build a moonshine still in the backwoods hills of southwest Portland. Much to his surprise he found that his coloring garnered him industry awards, unlike his feverish gathering of dry leaves for winter bedding. And he colors on.

Nate Piekos, letterer

NATE PIEKOS graduated with a BA in design from Rhode Island College in 1998. Since founding Blambot Comic Fonts & Lettering, he has created some of the industry's most popular typefaces and used them to letter comic books for nearly every major comic book publisher. Piekos's designs can also be seen on product packaging, on television, and in feature films.

Photos by Allan Amato